Rose Ruby

Story by Melaina Faranda

Illustrations by Cynthia Paul

Contents

Chapter 1

Rose Ruby

"Rose Ruby, are you listening?" Mr Grainger frowned. The way their teacher ran their names together made Rose and Ruby grin.

Rose and Ruby had always done everything together, ever since they had met on the first day of school. Together, as they sat on the story mat, they had learned "h" was for house, as well as for Hong, but Hong liked to be called Rose. That was the English word for her Vietnamese name.

They had started circus classes together, too. Rose was better at backflips, but Ruby was like a spider, climbing and spinning from the hanging silks.

At school, if Ruby had to create a cover page for a new topic, Rose did the drawings. But Ruby helped Rose with maths.

Mr Grainger told everyone to close their books. “We’re lucky to have a new student joining our class tomorrow,” he said. “It’s going to be a big change for Bella, moving here from the United Arab Emirates. She might be feeling shy, so I want all of us to give her a big welcome.”

He pointed to the empty chair next to Rose. “Rose, Ruby, I’d like you two to look after our new student, please.”

At lunch, Rose and Ruby talked about ways they could welcome the new girl.

"Maybe we could invite her back to my place and show her Nibbles?" Ruby suggested. Grandma had given Ruby the guinea pig when she moved in with Ruby and her mum.

Rose agreed. "And then we could go back to my place, and I could show her how to make Vietnamese coconut jelly."

Chapter 2

A Princess and Some Peacocks

The girls stared. Everything about Bella was . . . perfect. The new girl's shiny dark ponytail was held with a gold butterfly clasp. She wore expensive clothes from the kinds of shops that Rose and Ruby had only ever shuffled past with Ruby's mum on their way to a cheaper department store.

Bella smiled as she took the seat next to Rose, and neatly arranged her fancy stationery along the tabletop.

When the class did long division, Bella finished before anyone else. When it was time to draw the solar system, Bella's diagram was so good, Mr Grainger held it up to show the rest of the class.

Out in the playground at morning recess, Rose and Ruby were almost shoved aside. All the other girls and boys clustered around Bella, wanting to know more about what it was like to live in the United Arab Emirates.

"I had my own private teacher instead of going to school," Bella said.

She nibbled a slice of watermelon topped with chopped mint from her shiny lunchbox. "Sometimes, when my dad was working at the palace, I got to spend time with a princess. Her name was Leila, and she wore clothes that her mother bought from fashion shows in Paris," Bella added. "And for her birthday one time, all her family flew to Sweden in a private jet to stay in a hotel built out of ice."

"Wow – how lucky!" Freda exclaimed.

Bella smiled. “Leila loved it so much that her father had an ice rink built in the desert next to their palace. There were always peacocks wandering through the palace with workers running to clean up after them, or to deliver us snacks on big silver trays.”

“Wow, I thought that was something that only happened in the olden days,” said Leevin.

Bella blushed. “It’s different where we come from. There aren’t any palaces with teams of workers here. But there are housekeeping and chef services for the penthouse we’re living in.”

“What’s a penthouse?” Zoe asked.

“It’s an apartment on the top floor of a high-rise building,” said Rose. She knew that because she lived in a flat above her dad’s florist shop, with a balcony that looked out towards the distant city towers.

After that, Ruby felt shy about asking Bella if she wanted to come over to her cramped little house to play with Nibbles. And Rose worried that Bella would think Vietnamese coconut jelly was boring if she could just order anything she wanted from a chef.

But Bella smiled and chatted to both girls as if she thought they were already her friends.

Chapter 3

Secret Shame

There had been a cough going around the school. When Ruby got off the bus in the afternoon, Grandma stopped mid-hug to feel Ruby's forehead. "You have a temperature," said Grandma. "Let's get you straight to bed!"

Ruby felt too sick to argue. She fed Nibbles some carrot tops then flopped onto her bed. Later, she heard Mum tiptoeing into her room after work. Mum looked worried.

“It’s okay,” Ruby said. “I’m not that sick!”

Mum put her face in her hands and sighed. Since Ruby’s dad had lost his job, she needed to work extra hours to pay the bills. Today, she told Ruby, her mobile phone had smashed on the tiles. While it was being fixed, she wouldn’t be able to get any calls or messages.

Ruby hugged her mum. "If you like, I can stop going to circus lessons for a while, so you don't have to pay for them?"

Mum shook her head. "Ruby, you really are my gem. But don't you worry, we'll be all right. It's just one of those days."

On Monday morning, Ruby was excited to be going back to school. She had been sick for nearly a week!

Rose was already on the bus. "You got well in time for Bella's pool party this weekend," said Rose. "She's invited all the kids in the class. She said there's a water slide and the pool has a big glass wall so you can see the city below!"

Ruby couldn't wait to see Bella's penthouse pool. All day, she waited for Bella to ask her to the party too, but Bella didn't. Instead, Bella loaned her colouring pencils to Rose for the book they were making together about a zoo.

All the girls were talking about Bella's party during lunchtime, but Ruby still hadn't been invited. She tried to smile and nod along with the others, but the secret shame that everyone in the class had been invited except her sat in her belly like a heavy stone.

That afternoon, during her circus lesson, Ruby dropped the juggling balls, and lost her balance so many times that the teacher, Rochelle, said she wasn't allowed on the silks. "It's too dangerous if you can't concentrate, Ruby," Rochelle added kindly. "Maybe it's because you're still not well?"

Ruby knew it wasn't that – she just felt miserable.

Chapter 4

A True Friend

For the next few days, everyone talked non-stop about Bella's party. Bella smiled and laughed as she and Rose continued working on their zoo book, until Ruby felt like a small dark shadow in Bella's golden glow.

On their way home from school, Rose said, "I told Bella about our circus lessons, and she wants to come, too. Don't you think that would be fun?"

Ruby's heart beat faster. "No," she said.

Rose stopped. "Why? I thought you liked Bella?"

Ruby turned so Rose couldn't see the hot tears sliding down her cheeks. "How can I like someone who invited everyone in the class to her party but me?"

Rose's eyes widened. "Bella didn't invite you? Well, if she didn't ask you, then I won't go either!"

Ruby looked closely at Rose. She knew how difficult it was for her best friend to say she wouldn't go to a party that was going to be the event of the year. "No, you should go, it's going to be fun."

Rose shook her head. "It's 'Rose Ruby' or neither of us."

Ruby felt a big lump rise in her throat. "I don't want you to miss out. You should go, Rose, and you can tell me what it's like."

Chapter 5

A Missed Message

Ruby trudged after her mother into the phone shop. Mum had thought it would be good for Rose to come out with her, saying it was a beautiful sunny day. *A good day for a pool party*, Ruby had secretly thought. She looked at all the fancy new phones they could never afford while waiting for Mum to get her repaired phone back.

There were a number of pings as Mum went through her text messages. "Ruby?" said Mum. "What's this about a girl called Bella and a pool party? Why didn't you tell me? It starts in an hour!"

Ruby had never got ready so quickly in her life.

When they got to the huge high-rise building Bella lived in, Ruby and her mum caught a special lift that only stopped at the top floor. Kids were dancing around in swimming costumes.

Bella came to greet her, beaming. "Ruby, you came! You were the only one at school not talking about my party. I thought you didn't want to come!"

Ruby told Bella about her mum's phone. "I'm so happy I'm here. Thanks for inviting me, Bella."

Rose ran up to Ruby and gave her a huge hug before turning to point out the pool with its glass wall and slide.

All around the apartment were big framed photos of Bella surrounded by peacocks – but there were no photos of Bella with friends.

Ruby didn't feel jealous as she skipped towards the pool with her best friend.

"Ready?" Rose asked Ruby, grabbing her hand.

Ruby grinned. "One, two, three!" they shouted as they dived into the water, together.